lulu's

LITTLE
LIBRARY

Written and Illustrated by

lulu's

LITTLE
LIBRARY

MEET THE
FARM ANIMALS

ON A CHEERFUL FARM, THERE LIVED A VARIETY OF FRIENDLY AND LIVELY ANIMALS.

LET'S MEET THEM ONE BY ONE AS THEY INTRODUCE THEMSELVES AND SHARE A GLIMPSE INTO THEIR FARM LIFE.

MOO-VELOUS TO SEE YOU ALL!
I'M DAISY, THE HAPPY COW.

MOOOOOO
MOOOOO

I LIVE IN A BIG BARN WITH OTHER COWS.
I PROVIDE MILK AND LOVE TO CHEW ON JUICY GREEN GRASS.

HI THERE!
I'M BELLA, THE FLUFFY BUNNY.

HOP

MUNCH

TWITCH

I HAVE A COZY HUTCH WHERE I HOP AND NIBBLE ON FRESH VEGETABLES.

I'M KNOWN FOR MY SOFT FUR AND CUTE TWITCHY NOSE.

HELLO THERE!
I'M HENRY, THE MIGHTY HORSE

NEIGH

NEIGH

I HAVE A SPACIOUS STABLE WHERE I SLEEP AND EAT HAY. I GALLOP THROUGH THE FIELDS AND GIVE RIDES TO KIDS.

OiNK, OiNK!
I'M PiNKY, THE PLAYFUL PiG.

OiNK

OiNK

I HAVE A MUDDY PEN WHERE I ROLL AND PLAY.

I LOVE TO EAT YUMMY SLOP AND TAKE REFRESHING MUD BATHS.

QUACK, QUACK!
I'M QUACKERS, THE FRIENDLY DUCK.

I HAVE A POND WHERE I PADDLE AND SPLASH. I WADDLE ON LAND AND LOVE TO FIND INSECTS AND TASTY TREATS.

PEEP, PEEP!
I'M LUCY, THE ADORABLE DUCKLING.

PEEP

PEEP

PEEP

I HAVE A COZY NEST NEAR THE POND WHERE I FOLLOW MY MOTHER. I LOVE SWIMMING AND EXPLORING MY FLUFFY WORLD.

GOOD MORNING, EVERYONE!
I'M CLUCKY, THE CHEERFUL CHICKEN.

I HAVE A COZY COOP WHERE I LAY DELICIOUS EGGS. I SCRATCH THE GROUND FOR TASTY BUGS AND SAY 'CLUCK' ALL DAY LONG.

COCK-A-DOODLE-DOO!
I'M RUSTY, THE PROUD ROOSTER.

COCK-A-DOODLE-DOO!

I HAVE A PERCH WHERE I WATCH OVER THE FARM. I WAKE
EVERYONE UP WITH MY CROWING AND ANNOUNCE THE START OF
A NEW DAY.

CHEEP, CHEEP!
I'M CHARLIE, THE CUTE LITTLE CHICK.

CHEEP

CHEEP

CHEEP

I AND THE OTHER CHICKS HAVE A COZY NEST WITH MOTHER HEN.
WE PECK AND CHIRP AS WE EXPLORE THE FARM.

HONK, HONK!
I'M GINA, THE NICE GOOSE.

I HAVE A POND WHERE I SWIM AND FLOAT. I GUARD THE FARM WITH MY LOUD HONKING AND HELP KEEP THE PESTS AWAY.

SQUAWK, SQUAWK!
I'M POLLY, THE MAJESTIC PEACOCK.

I HAVE A VIBRANT GARDEN WHERE I STRUT AND DISPLAY MY BEAUTIFUL FEATHERS. I BRING SPLASHES OF COLOR AND ELEGANCE TO THE FARM.

GOBBLE, GOBBLE!
I'M SAMMIE, THE CHARISMATIC TURKEY.

I HAVE A LIVELY STRUT AND A VIBRANT PRESENCE. WITH MY FEATHERS PROUDLY DISPLAYED, I BRING DELIGHT TO THE FARM.

CLACK, CLACK!
I'M STANLEY, THE ELEGANT STORK.

CLACK

CLACK

I HAVE A TALL NEST IN A TREE WHERE I BUILT MY HOUSE.
I SOAR GRACEFULLY THROUGH THE SKIES, EMBRACING THE
FREEDOM OF FLIGHT.

BAA, BAA!
I'M WOOLY, THE FLUFFY SHEEP.

I HAVE A COZY PEN WHERE I SLEEP AND GET SHEARED.
MY WOOL KEEPS ME WARM AND MAKES COZY SWEATERS.

BAAH, BAAH!
I'M LARRY, THE JOYFUL LAMB.

BAAH

IN MY WARM PEN, I CUDDLE WITH MY LOVING PARENTS. THEIR GENTLE PRESENCE AND WATCHFUL CARE GUIDE ME AS I EXPLORE THE WORLD.

GREETINGS, FOLKS!
I'M PATCHES, THE FUNNY GOAT.

MAAAA
MAAAAAA

I HAVE A PEN WHERE I CLIMB AND NIBBLE ON ANYTHING I CAN FIND. I LOVE TO JUMP AND EXPLORE THE FARM.

HELLO, FRIENDS!
I'M POLLY, THE JOLLY PONY.

NEEEEEIGH

I HAVE A CHARMING BARN WHERE I MUNCH ON FRESH HAY AND RELAX. I LOVE TO TROT AROUND AND ENJOY THE COMPANY OF CHILDREN. WITH EVERY STRIDE, I SPREAD JOY AND HAPPINESS.

BRAY, BRAY!
I'M EDDIE, THE CLEVER DONKEY.

I HAVE A COMFY SHELTER WHERE I RELAX AND BRAY.
I CARRY LOADS AND HELP FARMERS WITH THEIR WORK.

MOO!
I'M BENNY, THE STRONG BULL.

MOO

I HAVE A WIDE PASTURE WHERE I GRAZE AND KEEP WATCH OVER THE COWS. I'M KNOWN FOR MY IMPRESSIVE HORNS AND PROTECTIVE NATURE.

GREETINGS, FRIENDS!
I'M ALICE, THE CUTEST ALPACA.

I HAVE A LOVELY PASTURE WHERE I GRAZE ON FRESH GRASS. MY WOOLLY COAT KEEPS ME WARM, AND I'M KNOWN FOR MY GENTLE NATURE.

WOOF, WOOF!
I'M BUSTER, THE LOYAL FARM DOG.

I HAVE A COMFY DOGHOUSE WHERE I REST. I HELP THE FARMERS WITH HERDING AND KEEPING THE FARM SAFE.

MEOW!
I'M MAISIE, THE CURIOUS CAT.

MEEEOW

MEEOW

I HAVE A COZY CORNER IN THE BARN WHERE I SLEEP AND CHASE MICE. I LOVE TO PURR AND KEEP THE FARM FREE OF PESKY CRITTERS.

SQUEAK, SQUEAK!
I'M MANDY, THE TINY MOUSE.

I HAVE A COZY BURROW WHERE I SCURRY AND HIDE.
I'M ALWAYS BUSY SEARCHING FOR CRUMBS AND EXPLORING THE
FARM.

Made in the USA
Middletown, DE
19 November 2024

65038763R00029